THE UNDEAD GIRL

The Undead Girl

Only Zombie Human That Exists on Earth

Coco Herrera

FADI PUBLICATIONS

COPYRIGHT 2022

1

PROLOGUE

"My name is Eve. If you are watching this, I am sorry."

***

"We urge all citizens to remain indoors."

The words were tinged with fear, but the newscaster remained poised and professional. The scrolling text at the bottom of the screen was the same message that had been on the television for weeks, often displayed over regular programming at various times of the day.

WP-V01 spreads. Symptoms include: loss of taste, increased appetite, increased aggression, fever, clouding of the eyes, memory loss, blackouts, and eventual death. Remain indoors. If you think you or a loved one is infected, call your city's hotline.

"The virus is not airborne, however, we still urge all citizens to wear masks, sanitize, and stay indoors."

The silence in the room hung like a fog over us. I glanced at the rest of my family in turn, eliciting a forced smile from my dad. He was trying to remain optimistic, but I could see the tension at the corners of his eyes.

"I repeat. Do not leave your homes unless you are seeking medical attention."

The news had grown increasingly bleak, with field reporters hiding from the violence on the streets.

"If you or your loved ones are infected, seek medical care. There is hope."

What remained unsaid was the deadline on that offer. Yes, there was hope—as long as you sought help within the five-day window. After that ...

"If you are infected and have passed the deadline, please head to your nearest quarantine facility."

A map popped onto the screen marking these facilities for each city. Video footage showed some people lined up to be accepted by one such facility. It looked clean and heavily secured. The image panned to a person in military fatigues, armed to the teeth.

I knew that there was little to be done once the virus incubated past the 5-day mark. Those facilities were little more than slaughterhouses. Many who went there were aware of their impending execution. Those who weren't brave enough stayed home and burned themselves out—the symptoms reaching their peak before killing the host.

A near-apocalyptic event, turning the world upside down.

But the fear that gripped the city was short-lived.

Just as suddenly as it began, it ended.

Life went on.

2

CHAPTER 1: BAD BLOOD

There was a time when it was just humans. Living their standard, workaday lives. I was one of them.

It was different, it was easy, it was simple. This life as a human.

You don't really notice the little things unless you slow down, or pay attention. The taste of honey and milk. The taste of candies, pizza, and every other sidewalk cuisine.

Coffee, tea, alcohol or ice cream. There are things that you don't realize you're missing until it's gone. I used to be human, before all of this craziness.

Credits: Valeria Boltneva

But that's not me anymore. I have changed in the very, very literal sense of the word.

I somehow got infected like the rest of the city. Unlike them, however, I never fully turned.

We're not sure where the virus came from, but theories abound. Environmentalists place blame squarely on the changing climate and the thawing of permafrost. While scientists aren't in agreement as to the origins, they nevertheless managed to create a cure.

We didn't know where it came from, but we now knew what it did. The virus changed humans, changed their core physicality, and stripped them of what made humans human.

It changed everything about the infected. Certain senses were heightened, and others were muted. In a sense, it seemed to have sped up human evolution—if you could look at it that way.

Humanity changed, and it killed us. Not all of us—it spread too rapidly for that—but enough that life adapted around this new threat.

The virus gets into the system through touch, through bodily fluids, but not through the air. We were lucky on that account. The first wave of this new virus tore through the city like a flashfire, incinerating lives. The high, burning fever and rapid, uncontrollable spread is how it got its name.

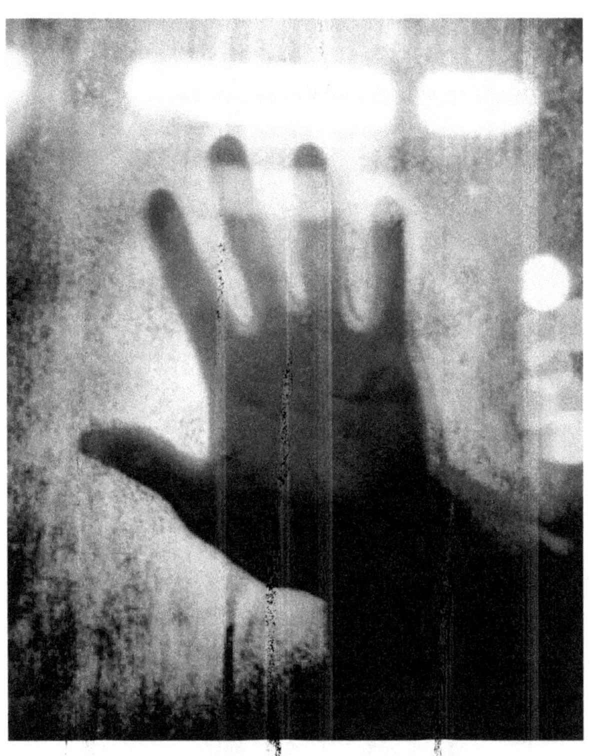

Credits: Josh Hild

It acted like wildfire, spread like wildfire. It was a flashfire of chaos, disease, and death. It burned through the host. It destroyed them and itself.

The second wave mutated and adapted.

I contain the second wave.

Just like the first wave, it changes the host. Unlike the first wave, the physiological changes are minute. Presumably the nervous system alterations are the same if not similar, excepting the fast mental deterioration.

The sharp gong of my alarm broke through my thoughts, alerting me that I had been awake and staring at the ceiling for some time. I blinked, my eyes burning from the still air.

My routine was pretty set, my body adapted to the pattern, now anticipating the clock instead of being startled by it.

I swung my legs over the side of the bed, aware of the short moment of disconnect as my body came upright. I inhaled deeply, feeling my lungs and chest expand as clean air filled them. I could feel the tightness as my muscles protested the overfilled organ and I exhaled.

I do the same thing each morning. It's my small way of making sure I'm still me. As long as I can still feel my arms and legs, and I can still breathe and move, the slow deterioration is less scary.

While there are less obvious physiological changes, I can feel them, like an ever-present shadow just out of range of the corner of your eye. Like a light touch, someone with too-cold hands holding onto the back of my brain, freezing it in place and at the same time, burning it from the inside out.

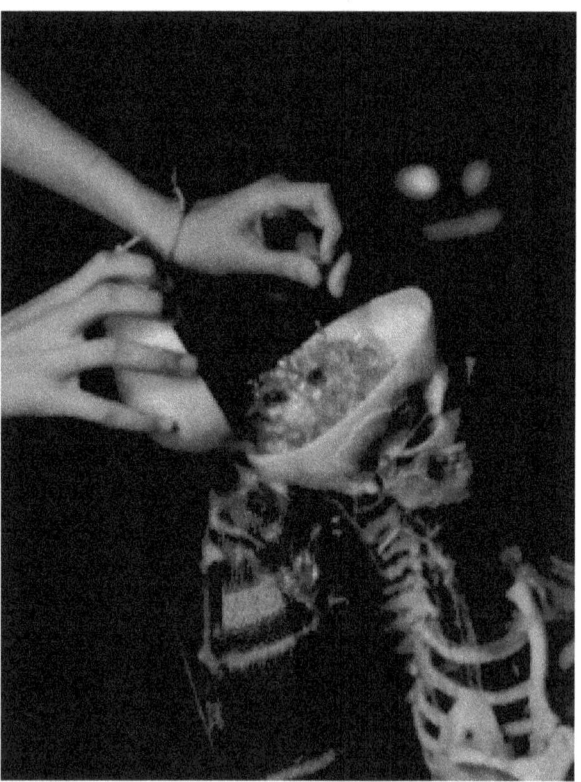

Credits: Cottonbro

That feeling is what keeps me careful.

I trim my nails and wear leather gloves, careful not to scratch. Whether it mattered or not wasn't the question. I just wasn't going to risk it.

I clean every surface thoroughly, wear a mask in public, and bring my own straw and cutlery to public places when that idiot Marcus insists on it.

I do the things normal humans do. I shop, I work, and I interact. I keep my relationships as simple as possible. No friends. No one gets close. Marcus is the only exception to that rule. Like a bad fungal infection, I never could shake him.

Only two things are vastly different. First, I do need food, but normal fare barely satiates me. Food tastes like ash. No matter what you mix it with, or how it's prepared. It still tastes like I'm licking the burnt side of a log. Sense of taste is muted, watered down with a note of "I should spit this out."

While the scent of brains sends delicious tingles down my spine and makes my mouth water at the mere thought of sinking my teeth into it, it is the texture that appeals to me the most.

It's soft and falls apart so easily, like perfectly prepared veal. I can get by on eating human food, but only barely. I know in time I'll need sustenance of the gray matter kind. I can feel it in my bones and in the back of my skull.

I take care to discard or burn anything that was contaminated with my blood. There are specialized dumping facilities where I take the biohazard containers and watch as they incinerate it. I am careful with my own fluids. Anything that could possibly come out of me gets monitored. There's no room in my life for love. I can't risk it.

I pull the sheets off my bed and take the large pile to the washroom. Boiling water and strong disinfectants make me feel safer.

Credits: Anna Shvets

I disinfect the toilet seat after using it and burn my dental floss. I toss my toothbrush in a cup with boiling water and bleach. I wash my hands until the skin is bright red and my skin tingles.

The same routine every day, unfailingly. One misstep and it will be over for humanity.

I can still feel. My nervous system is still intact, and for the most part, human-controlled.

I can still think, reveling in the ability to do so. I still have that part of my humanity, the part that we believe makes us human. That sense of "humanness" that brings us together in moments of distress. The same "humanness" that can tear us apart in those moments.

My emotions are still clear and unmuddled by the impending anger and violence. The thing that's missing, though, is the fear. And that scares me. Fear is what has kept humanity from extinction. A delicate balance of fear and bravery.

With one unchecked blood drop, or stray spray of fluid, I could easily destroy the world. No one would know the full repercussions until it was too late.

The first waves came like wildfire, whereas this new strain is more fluid, slower. It's like molten earth beneath the surface, slowly being brought to a boil, and it's burning away at me. I know there will be a day when I will turn into those things that hunger themselves out, there will be a day where nothing will satiate me and I will become the very thing humanity has fought to stave off.

3

CHAPTER 2: LIKE AN ITCH YOU CAN'T SCRATCH

It's a normal day out. I can hear the machine quietly thumping away as it runs through the hottest wash cycle, burning away any trace of my sweat. I have already opened the windows to my small apartment, allowing the cool, early-morning air to lazily bat at the curtains. The sun is creeping over the horizon and I clutch at my coffee mug, stilling the clinks made by the teaspoon I had left in there, the heat stabbing at my bare flesh.

Down on the street below, the usual early-risers are already at their day, hurrying to their tasks.

I watch as an elderly couple embrace and part ways. A twinge in my gut makes me turn away from the window. If I had wanted to, I could have continued my life as if nothing had changed.

I could have returned to my old life.

When the machine announces the end of its cycle, I follow its call. It has become a habit, a ritual. Get up, scrub down every surface, wash everything I wore or slept in. Shower and scrub until I am pink and tingling all over. Dress. And don't forget the gloves.

My phone buzzed, reminding me it was nearly time for work. I didn't need the reminder so much as the semblance of normality it brought with it. The constant ringing reconnected me to the world.

***

"Still?"

I flicked my gaze to him and smiled with my eyes, my muffled voice an affirmation.

I carefully folded and placed my casual wear into my locker. Inside a clear zippered bag. An extra layer of protection against accidental contact. I closed and snapped the lock.

"I don't understand you, Eve," Desmond said, still remarking on my face covering.

"Told you, Des, it's for your protection." I winked, trading my leather gloves for disposable ones. "Poor guy," I said, motioning toward the deceased on Des' table.

"Heart attack. Pretty standard fare for a fellow his size," he commented.

"Casket or cremation?"

"Cremation."

An excited little flutter started in my gut, and I swallowed.

I can't, I admonished loudly in my own brain.

"I'll get started," I said, my eyes taking stock of his pale, stiff form.

Fresh.

I inhaled, I could smell the fat and the flesh, and I salivated.

"Thanks," Des mumbled, not looking up from his paperwork. He would be finishing up his shift in a few minutes to get some much needed sleep.

Six months after the first wave we were still cleaning up the collateral. Many families had stockpiled food and self-medicated, often causing oversight on easily treatable illnesses. It led to fatalities like this guy.

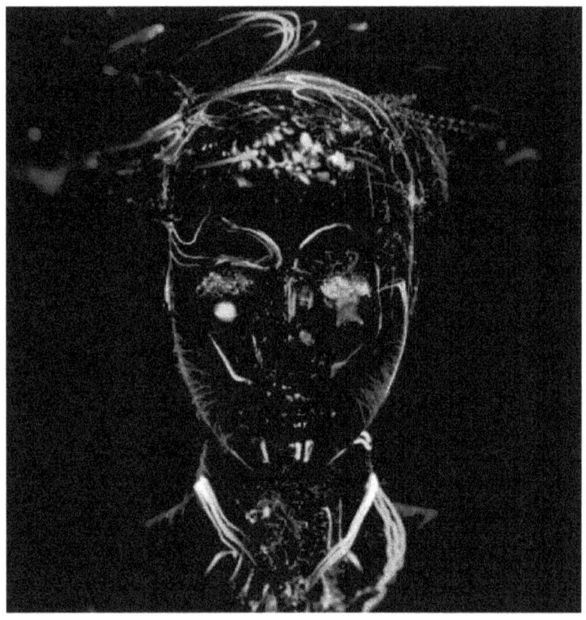

Credits: Sergey

I followed procedure, washing the body down. Although the autopsy had been completed by a different medical lab, we were blessed with the task of dressing up the corpses that graced Des' table.

Or, dressed them down, in the case of cremation, I thought.

I was starving, and my parasite brain could tell that food was nearby. Not the human-made swill, but the tender meat of a fresh meal.

I shoved the thought away, recoiling at the idea of sucking on his brain.

Des left with a comment about his daughter's recital, shrugging his large coat on before leaving me locked in with our new friend.

***

A vaccine had been made, spliced with the original strain and a handful of similarly acting viruses. The short lifespan of the original virus meant that for it to be effective, it required several applications accompanied by an aggressive course of antibiotics. Double whammy.

It ensured that there were more survivors than casualties. The vaccine was touted as a cure. After all, with a high success rate, and the alternative being death anyway? People were relieved.

The original strain was wiped out, along with twenty percent of the infected. Still, those odds were better than none, I thought.

I have noticed the change. It's not as fast as in the original, but it is there. There are far less negative side effects in the way of completely losing who I am.

There's still the heat in the back of my brain. The cold fire that became a constant companion hadn't appeared until I was recovering at my mom's house. We had all bunked together, watching the news and riding out the storm.

When we finally got treatment, a lot of those first weeks were a bit of a blur.

***

Marcus was seated across the table from me. Our bi-weekly coffee chat away from the listening walls.

"She's going to call my parents and set us up," he had said, laughing.

I groaned into my cup, "Don't even joke about that. She probably will."

It was already late summer, but the weather was promising an early snowfall. It was chilly enough that I was thankful for the gloves I always wore. The drawback of having poor circulation, I am cold to the touch. Not alarmingly cold, but enough to elicit touch from others in an attempt to warm the poor frozen girl.

"Marcus," I said quietly. "It's been nearly three months since you went on a real date. When are you going to take a study break and actually go out to meet someone?"

He laughed, looking pointedly at me, "How do you even know that?"

"That's neither here nor there," I said.

"I'm not planning on dating so much as finding someone to settle down with. I mean, isn't that what we all want?"

His answer surprised me somewhat. He sighed deeply, and I can smell the milk and sugar in his coffee from here. He always liked things too sweet.

Credits: Gagan Kaur

Curious, I think.

There was a brief moment where I found myself scanning his eyes. I knew looking for a sign of interest was futile. Even if he was interested in me, there would be no point to it. He changed the subject to the latest season of Destiny, a pretty decent sci-fi take on Shakespeare's life's work.

I sat there listening to him talk. I watched the way he moved, noted the color in his cheeks. I can see the life in him as he describes the space battles and the tense moments between the characters. Through his eyes I can feel the excitement and I get drawn in.

I can feel myself salivate and my body warm.

I stopped myself. He is human, and I am the monster under the bed.

I drank my coffee in silence as he continued to talk and gesture, and I suppressed the loneliness.

4

CHAPTER 3: SAYING GOODBYE TO DEATH

It started as a cold.

That's how it starts for everyone. Sniffles, inflamed mucosal membranes, and a general feeling of being unwell. It incubated for five days, showing little to no indication of being more than a seasonal cold.

In the end it took them ten days, ten days for the transformation to be complete, for their humanity to be burned away in a flashfire of pain and disease.

It took that long for the fever to burn out the host and turn into something half alive, and half something else.

It took those infected ten days to die, because none of their humanity remained to be saved—took them that long to be cursed to unliving. Sometimes I find myself thinking about them. Usually when I'm up to my elbows in soap and disinfectant, or when I'm fighting with my own humanity, staring down at a new body.

How I managed to survive is beyond me. How I still manage to survive is beyond me.

Along with the rest of the uninfected, I was taken to get a vaccine. I had holed up with my family when the stay-at-home order was issued.

I signed documents, had blood drawn, and lined up outside. Policed and watched. Most of us waited patiently, a few others were fearful and tense, demanding to be seen first, trying to push ahead of the crowd, but for the most part, we were eager to get this nightmare behind us. When my turn came, I got a needle in my arm, a course of antibiotics and dates for the next two doses.

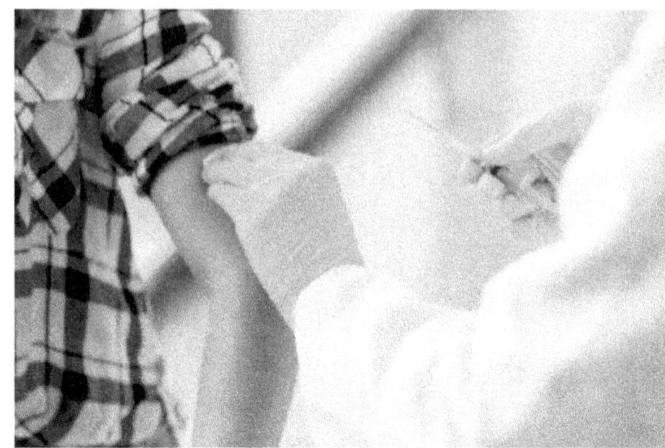

Credits: Gustavo

Two days later, when the second dose was due, I had a reaction to the vaccine. First it was light sensitivity, then escalated, and I was gone for five days.

I was trapped in a fever dream, seeing the flames lick at me, the faces of the dead eating me alive as I screamed without being able to make a sound. I was engulfed in flames and fear, and when I awoke, I had changed. It started as a cold.

When I got sick—a side effect, they had said, I became increasingly hungry. I ate just about everything, and created the strangest concoctions in the kitchen. Salt and vinegar chips on rolls, smothered in mayo and cheese whip. Slices of pickles on ice cream. I ate everything, but nothing tasted right.

I felt a strange kinship to the images of people they broadcast, as the last of the infected and turned were rounded up. The ones that would escape wouldn't last long. Too much time had passed, and they were beginning to starve.

They were hungry. And now they had turned on each other. It was horrific to watch. The camera would be at that unsettling offset angle, slightly distorted, almost like you're looking at the world through a fisheye lens. You could hear the screams. And when the camera crews fell, you could hear the sickening crunch, the wet thumps as their skulls were cracked open and their brains were removed.

The live teams were pulled from the red zones and the areas were sectioned off. Drones were used for surveillance, and soon enough, the lost souls of humanity stopped moving altogether.

I had gotten over my flu and taken the remaining doses while normality returned to the world around me.

***

I adapted. While eating was a chore now more than a pleasure, there was one thing that I couldn't quite shake the craving for. Human contact.

Touch.

I wanted to be held, I wanted to feel the rush of physical intimacy again and again, but I couldn't risk it. No matter how much I yearned and craved, I had forcefully denied every advance and every spike of desire when I went to a bar.

Credits: Sandeep

I couldn't afford to say yes, not with the uncertainty. I found myself staring at couples in the midst of their public displays of affection and would blush along with them, and I would angrily deny the emotions a chance to surface. Before long I began to avoid the places I had once enjoyed.

I look at the families and their young children, as they walk by going about their lives. It would be too easy to give in, too easy to say screw it and return the flirtations. Too easy to destroy the world with one kiss.

And at what cost? How long will I have them in my life? How long until my virus does to them what its predecessor did to countless others before me.

I don't know what's at the end of this phase. I can certainly venture a guess, and given the track record of those that came before me—my odds aren't great.

I don't know what the gnawing in my brain means, but I know that whatever it is, it's on a timer. How long until I turn on the people around me? On Des? On Marcus? Despite being cautious.

How long until hunger is the only thing I can feel and understand? That burning in the back of your brain that overrides everything.

5

CHAPTER 4: SOMETIMES WE NEED TO GET LOST

I haven't been successful in staving off the annoying hunger. The increase in appetite has certainly put a lot of strain on my already stressed-out system. I live as humans do, or try to. By eating their food, even though it's not quite as effective in sustaining me.

I can feel the desire for more than these tasteless meals, the *need* for more.

Have you ever felt something so deep inside you, like an itch several layers deep that you just can't scratch? A burning thirst in the middle of the night?

But this is deeper, and angrier, and more demanding.

At surface level it was a roiling, sickening feeling, that I knew something was missing. I knew something about that particular burn was dangerously different from just needing a glass of ice water.

I knew what I craved. I knew what I needed to do to quench it, but I couldn't do it. I had been living as a human, still felt human.

The last two years of my life I had managed to remain pure. Surprised? So am I. I didn't think I would make it this long. The first wave wiped themselves out, eventually turning on each other when there was no food left.

It had spread too fast, and it killed the host even faster.

What made Zexolia so dangerous is the way it acted. It is a virus that acts like a parasite. It spreads through fluid contact, or ingestion. It needs a healthy host to survive, but can survive outside the host for a number of days as it spreads. It is what made it so hard to control, and it's what made it so easy to contain. Once they knew the virus needed a healthy host and didn't survive host death, they developed their vaccines and antibiotics.

Once Zexolia bound to the host, it multiplied. Outside of the human host, the so-called offspring survived and were transported from host to host through sweat, blood, or saliva, protected by a thick protein sheath.

The virus didn't animate the dead.

It took over the living host and turned them into something that would be ... more. Something akin to undead.

Once the virus reaches the brain, once it binds with the nervous system, it spreads into the spine into every single nerve ending and organ. Accompanying this was the burning, like your very bones were turning to liquid inside your body. Burning that caused humans to go mad.

Burning away everything except the Wildfire and gnawing hunger.

6

CHAPTER 5: GNAWING HUNGER

The first thing I said when I woke from the fever dream was a snarky response to a stupid question.

"How do you feel?"

"With my hands," I had replied, groggy and annoyed from being woken.

The attending that had been monitoring my progress at the time had laughed at that response, and somehow, he had stuck around like a bad rash.

I had been the first non-lethal bad reaction to the vaccine they had seen. Assuming it was a combination of antibiotics and other drugs that reacted with my immune system, not too much was done except to stop the treatments until I was stable.

When I woke, they ran some standard blood tests and resumed the vaccine treatment. The initial reaction had seemed to simply be a fluke.

When the antibody test came back, showing acceptable growth and response rates, my case was closed and I was allowed to recover at home. But for weeks, months after the fact, after I was discharged and went home, this doctor had kept in touch.

"Marcus Wiles." He had offered his hand in greeting as I stared at him standing on my mother's porch. "It's nice to finally be able to talk in person. May I come in?"

The fact that he had been there and seen what I had gone through was a deciding factor—I had stepped aside and allowed him entry.

When I started realizing the truth about what had changed and why, I felt both relieved and tense at having him close.

I never told him about my official diagnosis. He didn't need to know, and my parents approved of having a doctor in the house. They had hoped he would rub off on me and I would return to school.

It didn't quite pan out. He came around more frequently and stayed for dinner on multiple occasions. Soon we became friends and I was relieved to have someone to confide in.

As he began specializing and our time became limited, he would bring his books to my house to study, often explaining procedures to me as a way to remember them.

"He's a good man, Evie," my mom would say, looking pointedly at the bare spot on my finger. I would roll my eyes and return to the study with refreshments. Many nights it ended with me falling asleep in one of the armchairs while Marcus pulled an all-nighter.

Yes, zombies need sleep. Not a lot, but our brains need rest, too.

Credits: Pixabay

I think my zombie brain and body mimics a human's perfectly, or as close to perfectly as it possibly can. Some sacrifices are made in exchange for enhancements in another area. Sacrifices need to be made somewhere. What I lose in taste I make up for in ability to go long periods without sleep. What I lost in eyesight I made up for in hearing.

I still needed sleep, and I still lived off of enough coffee to kill a horse. The one human habit I couldn't shake.

Once, after watching me make a third pot on a night of study, Mom had unsuccessfully tried to get me to switch to decaf. "The caffeine is going to kill you one day, Eve."

Marcus would make the same joke, teaming up with her and making other jokes at my expense. All good-natured, of course, but the ease with which he fit in scared me. My mom loved him. We became closer friends, and when he thought I wasn't looking I would catch him staring at me, as if he was trying to solve an incredibly difficult puzzle. Perhaps he was still concerned that I could, well, turn into one of those creatures.

If only he knew, I thought.

And in turn, I would watch him. I felt the familiar flutter in the pit of my stomach. Two swarms of butterflies warring with each other. One demanding I eat him, and the other—

I would blush and distract myself by making a fresh pot of coffee.

***

The thing that haunts me the most is the second biggest secret I have kept from my family. I had told Marcus only the bare basics, but not a soul knows about what I had done.

I knew with absolute certainty what I had become one chilly afternoon. I had needed to get away from the house that seemed to box me in. I had been alone at home, still halfway to recovery, looking after the family dog.

Bruno had been a stray, showing up at our house during the lockdown. We all grew quite attached.

I had left the door open, the dog got out, and in my haste to leave, well ...

I felt the small body shake the car when I pulled out of the driveway. My heart fluttered to a near complete stop. His pained yelp drew shivers down my spine.

Credits: Josh Hild

I gently placed him in the front seat and drove fast and hard to the nearest vet.

Bruno didn't make it.

And Bruno had been my first meal.

***

It really had been an accident.

I could feel without needing to look at him that he had died. His injuries had been too much. I was still racing down the side roads to the vet, avoiding places where I could get pulled over by the cops for speeding.

When I felt that shift, felt him go from barely there to gone, I glanced at him, suddenly filled with an overwhelming urge to pull over. So I did. I stopped on a side road next to a dry patch of land and sat in the car, listening to my own thrumming heart.

I took him into my lap and that's how we sat, together, on the sidewalk in ninety degree heat, and I sobbed. I sobbed because I knew what I was about to do. And I couldn't stop myself.

The funny thing that I would come to learn is that no food, no animal flesh or brain, tastes quite like a human's. Human was more filling.

It wasn't too long after Bruno that I had moved out to my own small apartment close to Des' mortuary.

7

CHAPTER 6: THE SLOW BURN

I have said before that I can still feel human emotion, and perhaps it's like the trade-off in my brain: the numbing of one sense in exchange for enhancement of the other.

I am struggling to keep it together. I am yearning for a man and a body I can't have. After Bruno ... I tried to stay away from people. I just couldn't stay away from him.

I wore my gloves, and I did little more than work and shop for necessities. I eat the scraps of the animals I find on the side of the road, and I struggle to keep it together when I'm prepping yet another corpse for burial. Des had come to trust me in his lab, leaving me and my potential for a meal unattended for hours at a time.

I simply couldn't do it. They were still human and I wanted to hold onto my humanity as long as I could.

I can't kill for my food and I can't turn anyone for companionship.

And what better partner than to have someone just like you?

Too easy, I thought.

Emotions are thick, and rich, and so volatile, and so completely wonderful. I wanted to have that new love feeling, that rush of being with someone new for the first time. At dawn, before the world awoke, and late at night, half-drunk and nothing mattered but the feel of another person's body.

With the yearning came the sadness.

And the loneliness.

I had to make that choice every time, to walk away. I couldn't risk it. There weren't going to be more of us—more of me. The end of humanity didn't seem like a preferable choice.

I remember watching all of these movies growing up. All those TV shows, and somehow, the zombies always turned out to be the bad guys ...

I found myself wondering if maybe all of this wasn't in my head, that maybe there was something else wrong with me—hoped that it was just a bad dream, that I was still stuck with that delirium and fever. Still stuck on the couch, getting better, and when I woke I would be normal again.

I don't want humanity to end. Because I know one way or the other, it will.

Whether I'm the next stage in the evolutionary chain, or if I am the disease that's going to wipe out the planet, I would be the catalyst that brings it all together.

***

I was driving a little too fast and a little too recklessly on the highway, looked down at the console to turn the radio up, and when I looked up again at the road, a metal barrier was coming at me.

I stupidly reacted in the only way I thought that would help. I jerked the steering wheel, flipping my car. It hit the barrier, crushed the roof of the car in on me, and I was aware of everything in slow motion.

I could feel the shards of metal piercing me. I could hear the engine wine as my foot was still down on the gas pedal. It whined in protest. I saw the car below me as my car flipped over the barrier, looking through the windshield I could see the unaware face of the driver—unaware of what was about to happen.

I cleared their car, hitting the road next to them hard, shards of car breaking off and scattering across the asphalt, flipping and rolling, and somehow managing to miss every single other driver on the road.

The car bounced again, finally shattering the windshield like a spiderweb. I couldn't see anything more than blurry shapes through the glass, like the veil between the living and the dead.

Credits: Guilherme Rossi

And then I went down into the ditch on the other side. I felt something hot, jarring, and I trembled. The adrenaline—I could hear my own breathing. Not really faster than normal ... just ... as if I was watching this from outside myself. Yet I could feel the tremors, and the blood rushing through me.

I hit the embankment on the other side, rolled and skid, kicking up clouds of dust, hearing metal on the stone, loud as if it was inside my own head.

When I came to a stop, the car with me trapped inside was enveloped in a cloud of smoke and dust. A moment of silence as the earth settled around me.

Then the sound returned. I could hear the cars on the road above and behind me, still speeding past. Screeching of tires as their slow human reactions responded to what they had just witnessed.

Time moved like congealed gravy, and I looked down, feeling blood pool in my lap. Metal shard of something sticking through my abdomen. My fingers danced over the surface, testing for pain and movement, the seam of my leather glove popped from the strain of holding onto the steering wheel.

With both hands I reached down and pulled.

I watched as dark blood flowed out like thick molasses before slowing, and then stopped.

I watched the blood congeal and clump around the wound. I held my hand over the wound, shivering, a new overwhelming hunger coming over me.

It was darker, it was more insistent, it was ... I could feel myself salivating and I swallowed. I could feel blood trickle down my face where I'd hit the side of the window and the steering wheel, and a face came into view over the side window above me. I could see a face staring down at me. I heard shouting in the distance, and all I could think in that moment was, that if I wanted to survive, I had to do what I had been designed to do.

I had to eat.

I remember laughing inside my own head, laughing at the ridiculousness of this thought, laughing at how easy it would be to step over that boundary.

8

CHAPTER 7: SCHOOL'S OUT

"Evelyn."

"Please, it's just Eve."

"Eve," she said, a twinge to her voice. "I've had a look at your transcripts." She paused expectantly. When it became clear to her that I wasn't going to interrupt, she continued.

"You dropped out of our program a few months ago."

I nodded.

"Why?" she asked.

"I changed my mind."

"You changed your mind?" She repeated my words slowly, as if trying to comprehend their meaning.

I nodded again. I knew she wanted more than what was written in my file. I was uncomfortable, unsure about how to answer her without it coming across as an absolute lie. I saw her expectant expression again and sighed.

"I got sick."

It was her turn to nod.

"I couldn't handle the workload, or keep up with my jobs to afford it, so I dropped out."

She looked over her notes, squinting, "You were the top–"

"Top five, yes I am aware."

"Why–" She stopped herself. "Your scores and performance were impressive. There would be no reason the school board couldn't make an exception for you once you got better."

I shifted in my seat, my hands clamped tightly together beneath the desk. How do you take the Hippocratic Oath when you carry the very thing that will wipe out humanity?

She looked at me over the rim of her glasses, the action making her look like a tense, angry librarian about to scold a noisy child. "Eve, we were made aware of your situation both by your parents and by you. We are just concerned that, perhaps, you might have acted too rashly. A bright girl–"

I shook my head to stop her but she continued anyway.

"A bright girl like you has a chance at a wonderful future," she said. "We could have had arrangements made, extra credit, I'm sure your professors would have been more than happy to have made certain concessions."

"My personal goals have changed," I said simply. "It was the better option rather than waste any more of anyone's time or money."

"If your goals have changed, perhaps you could have specialized in a different field, Eve."

"I don't know what I want anymore, is the point." I was irritated, her floral perfume choking my senses and burning my throat. "It is not a matter of funding, nor is it a matter of keeping up. As you have pointed out, I am a bright girl, and I catch up, even if I wanted to wait another six months. I can get a grant from this, or any other university, but I don't want to."

As I said those words out loud I saw her face change, leather squeaking as my grip tightened.

"I have worked several jobs earning to pay my way, both for school and other endeavors, and, to me, that was fine, because I wanted that–" I stopped myself.

"My goals have changed, and I expect you to accept and respect my choice."

A thick silence fell between us.

"I see," she said. "Are you sure?"

I nodded.

She made several notes, the pen scratching loudly on the paper. I waited.

Credits: Tima Miroshnichenko

At last she looked up at me, "If you are set on this decision, I would recommend you see one of our counselors before you completely take this step." She held up her hand. "I know. I just think that you might regret this choice."

"Talk to someone." She handed me a business card. "I've written her personal contact number on the back. Call her."

I didn't reach out to take it, so she placed it down in front of me on the polished desk. She tapped the card once before withdrawing her hand.

“Please,” she said, “we just want to be sure that you are certain of the sacrifice you’d be making.”

“Thank you,” I said quietly. “But I already know what I’m sacrificing.”

9

CHAPTER 8: RECONSTRUCTION AND REALITY

Like a lot of things that have changed in my life, I have sworn off going certain places and being in certain places. Being with certain people. When I came back from my undeath, my family knew I was different. Not exactly how different or in what sense of the word. They chalked it up to a near-death experience. I chalk it up to being dead. The world is silent because I can't hear my heartbeat. I know it's there, like a soft little thumb. Delete. From, delete, delete, like a soft thrumming not quite like a hummingbird's wings, but definitely not human.

I'm standing in the shower. I relish the feel of the water hitting me, the feel of the heat as it scalds my skin. It is relaxing, it is comforting. I look down at my hands and I notice that there's a blister forming on one of my finger pads. I squint, the steam rising around me, enveloping me.

When did I get this? I think.

I lightly tap the spot, pressing my thumb and forefinger together.

It doesn't feel particularly painful, but it's definitely uncomfortable. It must have happened a few days ago, maybe yesterday, I decided.

***

"What's up?" Marcus asked. My thoughts suddenly scattered.

"I'm sorry, what?"

"You were in the middle of a sentence and you stopped talking. Are you okay?"

"Yeah, I'm okay. Just a little tired." I wave my hand at him, take a sip of my coffee and grimace.

Not enough honey, I think.

I reach for the bottle. I can see his eyebrows raise, a question formed, but he didn't ask it. I dribble honey into my coffee, asking him about his research and planned dissertation.

"I've got graphs to complete, and case studies to write up, and I wish I could just–"

I take a sip of my coffee as he talks, and I grimace. I reach for the bottle of honey. He raises his eyebrows.

"You've already done that," he says.

I stop halfway to my cup. There's a slight tremble to my fingers that I hope he doesn't notice.

"Yeah, I know," I say. "I think I'm coming down with a cold. It just needs a little kick."

"If you want a kick why not ask them to make it Irish." He waggled his brows at me and we laughed.

"No, it's still too early for that, Marcus. Besides, you know I don't drink."

"Yeah, it was worth a shot. Seen you drunk, though." There's an indecipherable look on his face before it disappears. I shake it off, continue adding the honey and take another test sip. It's not great, but it is better.

A tense moment of silence passes. Marcus' dark eyes staring through me, my fingers running an outline on the bottle of honey.

"Maybe take some time off from work," he suggests.

I shrug, "I wouldn't know what to do with myself."

"Sleep?"

We laugh and the mood is lightened.

"Sleep would be good, but we both know I'd end up staying up late and not get any sleep in anyway."

"That's what you say now, just wait until your head hits the pillow and there's no alarm to wake you."

"I'm sure you'll be knocking at my door at dawn, trying to get me to write your introduction for you," I say.

He sniffed indignantly, pouting.

I laughed at him and our server brought out our desserts, our faux argument forgotten.

***

Goodnight, I say, my fingers tapping away at my phone screen. I don't bother waiting for a response. Marcus never replies after the first goodnight.

So, when my phone did tinkle, vibrating on the coffee table, I nearly dropped the kettle, spilling some water over the counter where I was making my cup of coffee.

I went to check and saw no notification. I stared at the screen for a minute, trying to figure out where that sound came from. That had definitely been my ringtone. And I absolutely heard it coming from the living room.

Placing the phone back down onto the coffee table, taking the ten steps back to where I had been, mumbling out loud to myself as I did so.

"Okay, you need to lay off the caffeine, 'cause you are hallucinating." I laugh awkwardly at my own joke, kind of wishing I had someone to share it with. My mind drifted to Marcus, and I felt a longing, a twinge of need to have him with me.

In any other circumstance I would have made a move by now, but not this time. Not like this, not while I'm—I lost my train of thought, walked back to the kitchen, picked up the kettle and noticed that it had gone cold.

"Yeah, you definitely need to lay off the caffeine, you might actually sleep a lot better, and stop freaking yourself out." I put the kettle back in its cradle, cold as I found it.

I couldn't really focus on anything for too long, I felt a little disconnected from myself as if my brain and body weren't communicating, as if there was a delay between what my brain said and when my body would perform the action. An alarming flutter started in the pit of my stomach, but I ignored it.

"Paranoid and overtired," I said, and finally crawled into bed, not bothering to turn off the light.

The next morning I woke, groggy and disoriented, and with a headache so big that it felt like it was splitting my skull into two.

"What the hell did I do?" I asked myself.

I take stock of my surroundings as I let myself adjust to the vertical position.

It's not terribly different but something feels slightly off, like when you rearrange your living room and the coffee table is just slightly unaligned with where it should be. It's off-center just enough to where you just walk into it at shin height and give yourself a bruise in the middle of the night, because you're too lazy to switch on the light when you want to get a drink of water.

Yeah, like that.

I couldn't put my finger on it.

I stumbled to the bathroom, still disoriented. I know this is my home. I can smell that it's my home. It smells like the soaps and detergent I use. I splash cold water on my face, trying to warm my fingers and bring a little color back into my tired face.

The blister has healed almost completely. I rub my thumb and forefinger together over the small bump. My nails look a little ragged, the edges uneven and unkempt. I immediately reach for the nail brush and clippers, annoyed at my inattentiveness.

Maybe Marcus is right, I thought. I need to take some time off. Maybe binge watch something on Netflix for a week and sleep until late afternoon.

I wiped down the sink and counter, soaking the tools in boiling water and bleach. I finally make my way down the carpeted hallway.

That feeling again. I find myself walking to the kettle on autopilot. A habit I couldn't quite break, I still craved caffeine. I touch the cold metal surface of the kettle—still cold from where I'd left it the night before.

I fill it with water, replace it in its cradle and hit the button, and wait, listening as the element heated up. I can smell the coffee, the scent lingering in the air. It was faint, and I chalked it up to eager anticipation of my next dose.

The scent again. Definitely not a phantom memory. I smell coffee. I hunt around in the living room, sniffing the air. On my coffee table is a half drank, ice-cold cup of coffee. Next to it stood a second. The white mug mocking me. I reached out to it, my fingers trembling.

The kettle clicked loudly as it reached boiling point and I jumped back guiltily, making contact with the wall behind me. My heel made contact with something soft. I knotted my fingers together, and glanced down.

Clothes. *My* clothes. Strewn in awkward, haphazard piles.

I slid down the wall, my hands in my hair, trying to steady my breathing. Tears were streaming down my face as I mumbled under my breath.

"No, no. Not now. Not yet."

10

CHAPTER 9: THE MISSING PIECES

I sit quietly and stare into nothingness, listening to the strange thrumming of my heart. It sounds less panicked and more like it's starting up a rhythm of its own.

I grew to like the sound of my changed heart. It was soothing, because it meant I was still me, despite the changes I could feel creeping up on me. It meant I was still alive.

Because you can't be a zombie if you're alive, right?

I take a sip of my coffee. It's cold and I stare into the inky darkness.

I stand in the kitchen with the kettle in my hand, now staring at the empty mug.

I can feel my breathing hitch into my throat because I can't remember what I was doing. I carefully return the kettle to its cradle and step back, clasping my trembling hands together as I struggle with my memory.

I think for the first time, I feel fear. I sit on the edge of my bed. Naked and wet from a shower I don't remember taking. There's a scent in the air. It is vaguely familiar with a tinge of iron, but more alive.

I sat against the wall, tears streaming down my face as I mumbled under my breath. My knees were drawn up to my chest, my hands in my hair gripping so tightly that I know it has to hurt but I can't feel it.

When I pull my hands away I can barely focus on the clumps between my fingers. It has lost some of its luster, losing that healthy shine. I close my eyes.

I stand again in the kitchen with the kettle in my hand, inhaling the fresh scent of coffee. I return the kettle to its cradle, stirring lots of honey into too strong coffee, because that's the only way I can taste it.

Vaguely the ring of my alarm notifies me of the time.

Again there's this alarming flutter in my belly as I finally realize something's wrong. Marcus—how long ago had we had our coffee date? Yesterday? Last week? I look at the calendar on my phone, only to see the waiting messages from Marcus.

I sent Marcus a quick text.

Sorry. Got caught up with something. I'll get back to you. I toss my phone onto the couch.

I squeeze my eyes shut, panic setting in. The feeling made me uncomfortable. It was alien to me.

"Just clean," I said. "Just like every day." I begin the routine of cleaning up my apartment. Clothing and linen into the washing machine. Dishes washed, dried, and packed away. Every surface disinfected. The carpet vacuumed. The bathroom disinfected and the floors washed with strong-smelling chemicals.

I stood in the shower, inspecting myself for scratches, bruises, or open wounds. No new blisters had appeared. I brushed my hair, being sure to catch the loose strands and throwing them in the steel bowl for incineration.

My memory comes back in a flash: I hold the kettle in my hand, startled by something, fumbling and pouring the boiling water over my finger.

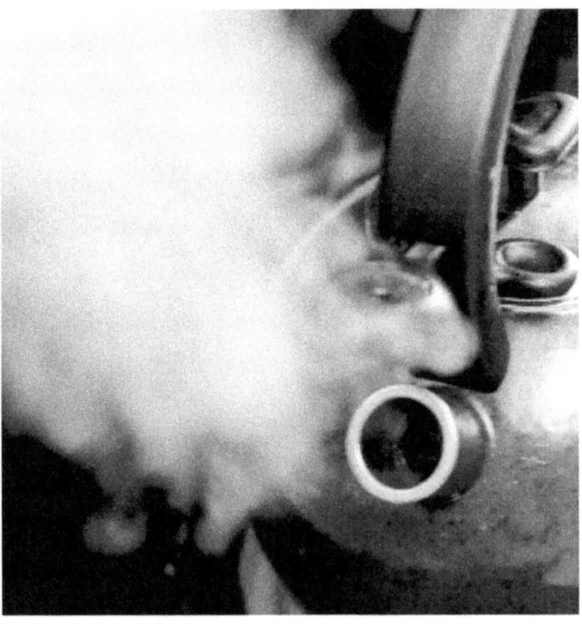

Credits: Barbara Webb

The shower was long and hot, steam thick in the room. Wrapped in a fresh, clean robe. I survey the rooms, my eyes drifting over every surface. It's clean and I feel my sense of normalcy return. I exhale a sigh of relief.

The kettle clicks and as the bubbles start dying down, I decide to send a message to Des.

Feeling a little under the weather. If you don't need me urgently, I'll only be coming in tomorrow.

Half a minute later I got a reply from him asking if I'm okay, telling me to get well, to message him if anything happens. I smiled, strangely pleased by the concern in his messages.

***

"I'm coming over," he said.

"No, M—"

"Stop fighting me on this. Des says you haven't been in for work in a few days. I'm coming to check on you." He hung up.

A few days?

No, that can't be. I had *just* messaged him.

11

CHAPTER 10: PLAYING CARDS WITH THE DEVIL

He doesn't know how strong I am.

Maybe he never bothered to test that, I think, analyzing him as my other hand wraps around his wrists. I can feel the bones beneath his skin as they move, protesting against the pressure.

The back of my brain is on fire. I can feel it coursing down my spine, lighting up.

"Why?" I managed to say, half growl, half sob, tears leaving salted trails down my cheeks. The word demands and pleads, but it doesn't quite convey every single emotion inside of me as much as my bare teeth and tear-streaked face does.

My teeth are bared, and my nails still digging into the palm of my skin, the tendons tight, the skin pale at the contact points as blood rushes through me.

The fire, oh, the fire.

His eyes flick to his wrist in my hand, and to my face. He is mentally making notes, calculating. I can feel my nails digging into the skin on his wrist as his bones creak beneath my grip.

If I had paid closer attention.

If *only* I paid closer attention, I lamented, the emotions congealing together, despair and anger.

***

"I was trying to help," Marcus said.

"Help." I said the word slowly as if I was testing the weight of it on my tongue, "What do you mean help? Help how, Marcus? Please explain to me how you thought this was helping?"

I didn't give him a chance to respond.

"I was just an experiment to you." I couldn't keep the hurt from my voice.

"Listen, listen," he said, the tone the same as every lecture he had given me. It irritated my already thin self-control.

"I didn't – I didn't do it on purpose." Marcus held his free hand up between us, his eyes flicking to his wrist, then back at my face, his expression changing to fear.

"It was my assignment to watch you, for the first few weeks, anyway, to see if there were any side effects. It was standard procedure."

Marcus continued, his voice now pleading, pressured by the silence, "Your reaction to the vaccine was something we hadn't seen yet, and it seemed as though you would have ended in the twenty percent.

"When they discharged you, I–"

"So you decided that I needed a babysitter?"

"No, I was curious–" Marcus looked guilty.

"What did you do?" I asked, the tremble in my voice gone, replaced by that fearless calm.

"About six months into your recovery, I administered the vaccine to you again," he said. "It was modified."

I could feel sinking throughout my entire body like my limbs suddenly became much too heavy to hold up.

"You did this while I was sleeping." Not a question.

He nodded, and a spike of adrenaline went through me. I forced myself under control. Retreating into my mind like I had taught myself, to pull back on the aggression and building violence. I couldn't form words, my face losing the contortions of emotion, smoothing out as I stilled my inner anger.

"Listen," Marcus said again. What was once an endearing quirk brought fresh irritation. "I can't take back what I did. It was under assignment—I was meant to watch you—just watch you."

His words flowed faster, more urgent, as if overwhelming me with them would change the tide.

"I wrote a paper about it," he said, "And I just—that was it. That was the end of it and then I just–" He cut himself off, squeezing his eyes shut, hating the words he was speaking.

"I couldn't contain my curiosity. I had to know why you reacted that way. The physiological changes, your seeming disinterest in food, even your cleaning habits. It all spoke volumes of something deeper.

"They had drawn blood in case they had to run additional tests, but when your condition improved–" he paused, "I stole the samples."

"You what?" I felt the cool, calm anger explode and roil, turning dangerously volatile. I dropped his hand and stepped away from him.

"No one realized that you were immune."

I stared at him as the words hit home.

"The vaccine didn't quite react as predicted. I ran my own tests." His eyes lit up. "I'm not the best at it, but have you seen how amazing lab work is? We had vials, or at least,

I knew people who had vials of the original infection. Blood drawn from those too far gone to save."

All that infected blood, I thought. Where was security in all of this?

The more he spoke, the more animated he became. He started pacing, grinning. He had this manic look to him.

"I experimented," he said. "I recreated the virus. I experimented because I couldn't figure out why you had reacted that way. After administering the second dose, I expected more of the same, but it never came. I just had to know!"

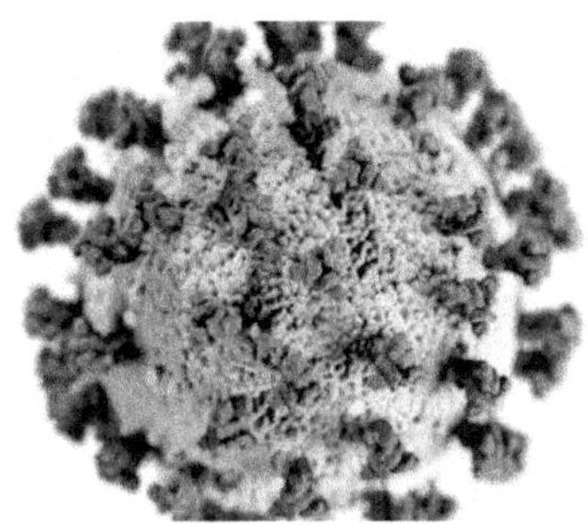

Credits: CDC

He turned to face me, his eyes bright, "When I figured out you were immune, I didn't tell anyone. If they found out I ran unsanctioned experiments on you I would have lost my license. I would never be able to finish my degree, I would never be able to practice again ever. I have wanted my whole life to make a difference—"

"You thought you could make the difference with me," I said quietly. "You thought I was your ticket to the big time."

Marcus was quiet for a few seconds. His mania deflating a little. He took a deep breath and he sighed. "It's not that easy to explain. I thought you were just another test subject, and when I realized what was actually happening was you—

"At first I was just scared for humanity. Waiting for the right moment. I wanted to save the world, and what better way than already having a vaccine for your strain?" he said.

"If we could make a new, better vaccine, before the virus even spread—we could have made millions!"

"You did this for greed?"

Marcus ignored me, too caught up in finally being able to tell someone about his brilliant plan. "The more I experimented, the more I learned. I was so close. Then your blood stopped reacting. It stopped doing weird shit in the labs and I figured that was the end of it, I figured it was just that.

"I was devastated. So I did the unthinkable."

I barely hear him over the whistle in my ears, tears rolling silently, drawing out the carefully bottled emotions.

"I administered my half-finished vaccine. Your blood reacted in the same way as it had the first time, except it mutated again."

"You did this?" I was choking on my words. "You gave me a broken, mutated strain? I lost time! I could have hurt people!"

He held up his hands in defense. "I am sorry for hurting you, but I am not sorry for what I did. I had humanity's best interests at heart."

"No," I said. "You had your own best interests at heart, making millions off—" I stopped, trying to reign in my emotions and failing.

"Things seemed okay for a while. It was small things, like forgetting that you'd already made coffee, or that you'd already told me a story. It's like you went through cycles, these phases, and then it happened more frequently—"

"Stop talking, Marcus," I warned him.

"—and when you walked away from the car accident that should have killed you, I finally saw a better solution, a better way ..." He trailed off. I stared at him, trying to piece his words together, my memory replaying the very same accident, over and over in my head.

I looked at him for a very long moment, and that's when I realized *why* it had been easier to resist him. The parasite in the back of my brain didn't want him because he was like me. He held a part of my virus inside of his still-human body, slowly changing the way he smelled to me, until he became all but invisible to that same part of me.

Anger and sadness mingled inside of me, forming a different kind of fire. Like the ticking of a clock, like a bomb waiting to go off.

"Listen," Marcus said. "I – you're not alone anymore. I'm like you—"

I shook my head repeatedly, half laughing, half crying in complete frustration and disbelief. So many mixed emotions that I didn't know what was real, or what was mine. "Marcus, you don't understand. Why do you think I isolated myself? I don't *want* people to have this. It's not good."

"Think of the lives we can save!"

"You don't know what it's going to do to you!" My voice was shrill, all my restraint evaporating. "You've injected my blood into you!" I clenched my fists, feeling my heart shake my body. "You took my infection, my mutation, and just–"

"Stop it," he said.

"You don't know how you're going to react, you could end up like the others."

"Sto–"

"No! You did a dangerous, stupid thing, Marcus. You could lose yourself and infect people without restraint! You're gonna wipe out the human race for what? Immortality?"

Suddenly Marcus was angry, his lips pulled back over his teeth, and I could sense the same aggression in him that was in me—the aggression I was trying to suppress. He was going through it a lot faster than I had—his change was coming on faster.

12

EPILOGUE

For the first time since I'd turned, I was overcome by this flow of white, hot anger, burning through me more powerful than any emotion I've ever felt. Stronger than any emotion I had experienced with this parasite in the back of my brain.

Betrayal. Disbelief.

The anger felt good. It felt right, as if it was what I was craving above all else. The release of inhibitions and giving in to the violence.

He did it.

He stands in front of me with this half grin on his face, as if I should be proud of him. As if I should be amazed at how long he's kept the secret. Amazed at his brilliance.

My friend, a stranger.

Humanity is disgusting, I think.

A roar in my ears, the thrumming of my heart has overtaken me, pounding through me, filling me with adrenaline and purpose.

I feel an unfamiliar itch on the palms of my hands and I look down. I'm not wearing my gloves, my fingernails are biting into my skin but there's very little blood. I can't bring my muscles and tendons to relax my fist.

So I leave it clenched.

My breath hitches and I can't find my voice to yell at him, all I can do is growl. Slowly, comically, his pompous expression changes, and it is delightful to watch, as he realizes how tremendously he had fucked up.

I advance on him, my prey, lips drawn back over my teeth.

***

I was on my knees on the tiled floor of my little apartment, staring at the growing pool of blood seeping into the fabric of my jeans. I stared at the slivers of flesh still clinging to my fingernails, between my fingers, clumps in my hands.

I taste iron on my tongue and I lick my lips, even after wiping my face on the shoulder of my shirt, it was still there.

I look down at the greying pallor of Marcus's face. His fingers twitching as his still-intact brain tried to control what was left of him.

I took a steadying breath, inhaling the sweet, metal scent.

I held my hand over his face, feeling the soft contour of his features and the scratchy 5 o'clock shadow on his cheek. I turn him away from me, opening the back of his head to my gaze.

With my ragged nails I pierce the soft flesh and pull. The skin separated from the bone with a pop and a squelch. The exposed bone pale and inviting. Again the hunger set the back of my brain on fire. My stomach growled and my mouth watered.

A memory of Bruno popped into my head, the similarities startling. Just like before, I knew I had hit the point of no return. I gripped the face like a bowling ball, the instinct to feed overriding everything else. My fingers pushed past his eyes and I lifted the skull, smashing it against the tile, over and over again. I could feel his teeth cut my skin as my thumb pushed into the soft palate of his mouth.

My fingers found the soft veal-like flesh inside the hollow and I pulled it free, bringing it to my lips. It was all there was for me, this hunger and heat, and the promise of a warm meal.

I leaned into that feeling for a moment, not caring, only driven by need.

Thinking clearer than I ever had, I wiped the blood from my face with the hem of my shirt and began to separate flesh from bone.

***

I picked up my phone and turned on the camera, hitting the record button. I could see my wild image on the screen looking back at me. Tears were still flowing silently, creating streaks through Marcus' blood on my face. Somewhere inside of me the loneliness began to set in.

"My name is Eve. If you are watching this, I am no longer me. If you are watching this, I am sorry."